The Race for a
NEW LIFE

BY ALVIN ROBERT CUNNINGHAM

Perfection Learning®

Cover and Inside Illustrations: Dea Marks
Design: Emily J. Greazel

Dedication

To the loving memory of my late mother,
Lorene Cunningham, and younger brother, Pete Cunningham

About the Author

Alvin Robert Cunningham is a retired teacher from the Ottawa Elementary District in Ottawa, Illinois. He is now an author for Perfection Learning. He has written another chapter book, *A Letter for Mr. Lincoln*, and is currently writing a series of books for a social studies program.

Mr. Cunningham enjoys reading, especially about the Civil War and the American West. He likes watching birds and other wildlife. He also enjoys taking nature hikes and listening to good music.

Mr. Cunningham and his wife Rita enjoy living at their new home in Streator, Illinois.

Image Credits: © Bettmann/CORBIS: pp. 27, 41; © CORBIS: pp. 52, 57, 59; ArtToday (some images copyright www.arttoday.com): pp. 4, 9, 13, 15, 17, 19, 22, 26, 29, 30, 35, 40, 43, 58

Printed in the United States of America. For information, contact
Perfection Learning® Corporation, 1000 North Second Avenue,
P.O. Box 500, Logan, Iowa 51546-0500.
Tel: 1-800-831-4190 • Fax: 1-800-543-2745
perfectionlearning.com
PB ISBN-10: 0-7891-5856-6 ISBN-13: 978-0-7891-5856-7
RLB ISBN-10: 0-7569-0994-5 ISBN-13: 978-0-7569-0994-9

5 6 7 PP 17 16

TABLE OF CONTENTS

CHAPTER 1

"Move out of the way, kid!" shouted an angry voice.

Josh McCord stepped back. He kept his eyes closed. They burned from the swirling dust. He heard the sound of horses and wagon wheels.

Josh opened his eyes. A large freight wagon passed in front of him. Arkansas City, Kansas, was painted on its side.

His family had often talked about Arkansas City. It was the starting point for the race. People would **claim** land at the end of this race.

Josh was excited. That's why he and his father were in town. Their wagon was stacked with supplies. His grandfather's horse, Lightning, was tied to the back.

Josh was tall for his ten years. He could see his father talking to a soldier. Behind them, the sun was rising.

Then Josh noticed a sign with large letters. It hung on the side of a building.

Cherokee Strip Land Rush

Starts at noon on September 16, 1893

Register for certificates at booth 9

Josh had never seen so many people. He guessed they had come for tomorrow's race too.

Josh thought about the family farm in northern Kansas. He remembered his family waving good-bye.

Mother had been holding baby Jenny. Grandpa Henry had been next to her. He had been waving the only arm he had. The other had been **amputated** during the Civil War. Next to Grandpa stood Uncle Nate. The black man wasn't Josh's real uncle. He'd been with Josh's grandfather since the war.

Uncle Nate had been a slave in the Indian Territory. During a battle against the **Confederates**, Josh's grandfather had rescued Nate.

Josh loved his entire family. He looked forward to seeing them soon.

"Best be watching for Joseph Eagle Claw's sons," Josh's father said.

Josh turned to watch his father. Mr. McCord opened a **tarp**. He tied it to a nearby tree

"It will give the horses some shade," he said.

Josh's father wiped his forehead. "It's going to be another hot one today. And that registration line looks mighty long."

Josh looked again at the people around him. Some were riding in buggies or wagons. Others were on horseback.

Many people walked around with handkerchiefs over their mouths. One man even wore goggles. The blowing dust was terrible.

Then Josh thought about Joseph Eagle Claw. He was a Cherokee. He and Grandpa Henry had fought with the **Union** army in the Civil War. They had remained good friends.

Two 160-acre **homesteads** were next to Joseph's property. It was more land than Josh's family had now. And the new land's soil was very **rich**.

Joseph Eagle Claw wanted Josh's grandfather and father to claim that land. Then he would help Josh's family start a new life.

CHAPTER 2

"Son, bring Lightning over here,"
Mr. McCord said.

"Yes, Pa," answered Josh. He untied
Lightning's rope **halter**. The saddle and
bridle were in the wagon.

Grandpa Henry wanted them to have
a riding horse. Lightning would be
needed after they **staked their claim**.
Mr. McCord would ride the horse to the
land office.

Josh whispered in the horse's ear. "It
will be cooler for you under the tarp."

Josh had been riding Lightning for a long time. Lightning was the grandson of the horse Grandpa Henry rode in the Union **cavalry**.

"Talk to Lightning from your heart," Grandpa Henry had told Josh. "Then he'll run faster. And he'll protect you." Grandpa often reminded Josh that Lightning's grandpa had saved his life many times.

Josh's father never believed those stories. "Your grandfather's getting old," he would say. "Don't pay attention to that make-believe stuff he tells you." But Josh was pretty sure Grandpa's stories were true.

"Daniel McCord, is that you?" a voice asked.

Josh looked up. His father was shaking hands with two men.

"Josh, meet David Trotting Wolf and John Fishing Hawk," Mr. McCord said. "They're Joseph Eagle Claw's sons."

Josh walked over and shook their hands.

"It's very nice to meet you," David said.

"You look just like your father," John added.

Josh was surprised. They looked like Indians. But they didn't sound like other Indians he had met.

"Son, remember when your grandfather and I rode down to visit Joseph Eagle Claw?" Mr. McCord asked. "It was six months ago. That's when I met David and John. They showed us the two homesteads we'll try to claim."

The two Indians tied their horses to the wagon.

Mr. McCord paused and put on his wide-brimmed hat. "John is going with me to the registration line."

Mr. McCord handed John some papers. "John will claim one homestead for your grandfather. He can do that for a Civil War veteran."

"And we'll stake the other claim, Pa?" asked Josh.

"If we're the first ones there. And if we're the first to file the claim," his father answered.

Mr. McCord looked at his friends. "We've already sold our small farm," he explained. "We didn't receive much since the land's **played out**. But we did make enough for the homestead fee."

Mr. McCord pointed to the tarp. "I bought a fine team of horses," he said. "I've been training them every day for the race."

"But what happens if we're not first, Pa?" asked Josh. "What happens if we can't claim the land?"

"Our family will just move farther west, son," his father answered. "And we'll look for some other good land to buy."

Mr. McCord looked at John. "We'd better leave now. That line's long. Let's hope we're back before nightfall."

Josh watched them walk away.

CHAPTER 3

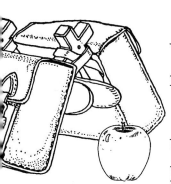

David took some fruit and water from his saddlebag. He reached for his rifle too.

David and Josh climbed up to the wagon seat. David handed Josh an apple. Josh took a bite. Then he took a drink of warm water.

Suddenly, David stood. He held the rifle in front of him. "Best stay clear of those horses, mister!" he yelled.

Josh saw a man step back from the tarp. He gave David a mean look. But he turned and walked away.

David sat back down. "Has your grandfather ever told you what happened during the war?"

Josh tried to answer, but he coughed instead. "What is that *smell*?" he asked.

"It's smoke," answered David. "They're burning off the tall prairie grass before the race. It's a bad idea with this many people around. But the burned ground will be easier to travel across."

Josh looked back at David. "My grandfather doesn't talk about the war much. He says too many bad things happened."

"That's true," said David. "But one good thing *did* happen."

Josh looked up at David.

"Your grandfather saved my father's life." David smiled. "Let me explain. My father joined the 1st Indian Home Guard. It was made up of loyal Cherokee.

"My mother, brother, and I followed our father to Kansas," he continued. "There, the Home Guard joined the 9th Kansas Cavalry."

"That's what Grandpa Henry was in," said Josh.

"How did you know?" asked David.

"It's on Grandpa's saddle," answered Josh. "It's the one I use with Lightning."

David continued. "The soldiers went to my people's land. And they fought an important battle there. It was at Locust Grove."

"That's where Grandpa rescued Uncle Nate." Josh remembered the story his mother had told him.

"And that's where the Confederates had my father's group **pinned down**," added David. "Many Cherokee were killed. My father's horse was shot. And Father was unconscious."

Then David put his arm around Josh. "And that's when your grandfather was a hero," David said. "He rode his horse through cannon and musket fire. He reached my father. He put him over his horse and brought him back to safety."

"Is that when Grandpa lost his arm?" asked Josh.

"Yes," answered David. "He received a bad wound. His arm had to be amputated."

David patted Josh's shoulder. "The Union cavalry gave your grandpa his horse and saddle. It was for his bravery."

Then David smiled. "And my father made him his brother for life."

CHAPTER 4

It was evening when Josh's father and John finally returned.

"Hello, Pa," said Josh.

"How did everything go?" asked David

"We were lucky," answered John. "More help arrived when we got there. The lines moved faster."

"We both registered," Mr. McCord added. "And we both bought **certificates**."

Mr. McCord shook his head. "You can't believe the heat and dust down there. One old man died this morning. He'd been in the line since yesterday."

"And two men were arrested," John added. "They were selling fake certificates."

"What do we do now?" asked David.

Mr. McCord took off his hat. He wiped his brow with his handkerchief. "They told us to take our **gear** closer to the starting line. We'll camp there tonight."

Josh helped his father. They put the team back in the harness. They pulled the tarp back over the supplies. Josh tied Lightning to the back of the wagon.

Josh climbed into the seat next to his father. David and John mounted their horses. The four rode down to the camping area. They found an open spot near the Arkansas River.

In the twilight, campfires glowed in both directions. Josh could hear people talking and singing.

The four set up their campsite and ate supper. Mr. McCord tied the team to the side of the wagon. John and David tied their horses to a tree.

Josh and the others unrolled their blankets. Josh's blanket was between John's and his father's.

"I'll stay up and keep the fire going," said Mr. McCord. "I'll wake you early. And we'll talk about our plans for the race. Then we'll go to the starting line. The race begins at noon."

Josh was tired. He stretched out on his blanket. He quickly fell into a deep sleep.

CHAPTER 5

The horses' neighing woke Josh. It was early morning. He was cold. He saw that the fire was almost out.

The team horses were excited. They were pulling at their halter ropes and rearing. Josh thought he saw an outline of a man.

"What's going on over there?" yelled Mr. McCord.

Josh watched as his father stood and ran to the horses. John and David ran in that direction too. They carried their rifles.

In the darkness, Josh heard the men shouting. He was scared!

Then his father appeared in the firelight. John was wrapping a cloth around Mr. McCord's hand. It was bleeding!

"It's all my fault!" exclaimed Mr. McCord. "I should have stayed awake! I was supposed to watch the horses!"

David joined them. "It's no use," he said. "One of your team was stolen. And the thief is gone."

Josh slowly stood up. He walked over to his father. "Are you all right, Pa?" he asked.

"Yeah. I'm OK." Mr. McCord looked at his hand. "I tried to grab him. But he cut me with his knife."

He looked at Josh. "We can't do it now, son," he said. "I can't race the team with a horse missing. Especially with a bad hand!"

Josh said nothing. He thought about his grandfather. Then he stepped closer to his father. Josh looked up at him. "A McCord can *still* stake the claim!"

Mr. McCord's eyes met Josh's. "I can do it, Pa. I can ride Lightning."

Mr. McCord studied Josh's face. Then he shook his head. "No, son, I can't let

you do it," he said. "It would be too
dangerous."

"But Pa, you know what a good rider
I am! Grandpa has taught me everything
he knows!" Josh argued.

"I know that, son," his father said.
"But you won't know where—"

"Daniel," John interrupted. "He could
just follow me. We can take some
shortcuts to the land," he explained.
"It will be a difficult ride. But I think he
can do it."

David moved closer to Mr. McCord.
"And I'll harness my horse with the
team. They won't be as fast. But we'll
reach there soon enough."

Josh studied his father's face. He
thought he saw his father start to smile.

CHAPTER 6

Later that morning, Josh was nervous. The race would start soon. He tried to be calm.

Josh was in Grandpa's saddle. He could feel Lightning beneath him. Josh and Lightning were between John and his horse and the wagon. They were about four rows back from the front.

People crowded together. They pushed toward the starting line.

Josh heard arguing and cursing. He saw two men rolling on the ground, fighting.

Wagons of all shapes and sizes came into view. Josh saw people riding horses and mules. Some were riding bicycles. Others were on foot. He even saw one man riding a cow.

Everyone was trying to keep the animals calm. Josh could also see train cars. People filled the slow-moving trains. The dust and the noise were terrible!

Josh checked his stake strapped to his saddle. A flag was attached to it.

Mrs. McCord had made the flags for good luck. The words *9th Kansas Cavalry* was sewn on his. And *1st Indian Home Guard* was sewn on John's.

The start of the famous run of homesteaders into the Cherokee Strip, Indian Territory, in 1893

Josh felt his canteen belt. He opened the buttoned pocket. He made sure his certificate was still there.

"Josh," shouted John. "Be careful when the race starts. You don't know what you'll have to go around or jump over!"

"I will," Josh answered.

"It will take more than an hour of hard riding to reach the land!" yelled John. "We'll go slowly at first so our horses don't become **winded**. Then we'll **gallop** faster and separate from the pack."

"And, Josh!" Mr. McCord called.

Josh turned to his father. Mr. McCord held the **reins** in his bandaged hand. David was sitting next to him.

"Just follow John," Mr. McCord yelled. "Stake the claim where he tells you. Then wait for us. We'll get there as fast as we can. And be careful, son!"

"OK, Pa," Josh yelled back. Then he patted Lightning's neck. He bent closer to his ear.

"Just take it easy, boy," Josh said. "Just pretend it's a practice run at Grandpa's. You can do it, Lightning. This is the beginning of a new life for our whole family!"

Suddenly it became quieter. John pointed to a soldier. Josh saw the soldier look at his watch. Then he put a bugle to his lips. Other soldiers held their rifles in the air.

Suddenly, Josh heard a loud bugle note. It was followed by rifle shots.

The crowd in front of Josh burst over the starting line. They were soon lost in a cloud of black dust!

CHAPTER 7

It was their turn. Josh let John's horse go ahead of his. He followed it.

The black dust was clearing some. It smelled like the ashes of the burned prairie.

Now Josh heard the clatter of hooves. He heard the rattle of wagons.

Josh guided Lightning around an overturned wagon. He hung on to the saddle horn with one hand and crouched down. He tucked his knees into Lightning's sides. Lightning quickly jumped over a man on the ground. He'd been thrown from his horse.

"Good jump, Lightning!" shouted Josh. "I knew you could do it!" He was still following John's **pinto**. He could easily see its white spots.

The crowd began to spread out. But Josh couldn't see his father's wagon. He hoped nothing had happened to it.

Josh tried to slow Lightning to a gallop. He wanted the horse in a good rhythm. Grandpa had told him a gallop was the best **gait** for long-distance riding.

"That's it, Lightning," said Josh. "Just take it nice and easy." He could feel Grandpa's horse relax. Josh always liked Lightning's galloping rhythm.

"Josh!" John turned in his saddle. "Bring your horse closer to me."

Josh rode Lightning up to John. He could see the dust from the horses in front of him. They were running in all directions.

"Are you all right?" asked John. "I saw you make that jump back there."

"I'm OK," answered Josh.

"We'll keep going this direction. And we'll keep this same pace," John yelled. "We'll ride for quite a while. Then we'll cut to the left."

Josh watched the land carefully. He guided Lightning around the many prairie dog holes. He soon lost track of time.

"Josh, let's cut to the left now," yelled John.

They separated from the other riders. They rode for about 20 minutes.

The two carefully climbed down a steep hill. Then they crossed a stream. They entered a meadow. It had good land all around it.

"Josh, stop at that section marker." John pointed ahead of him.

At the section marker, John gave Josh a piece of paper. "Put that with your certificate," he said. "Your claim is the southwest quarter of section 8. Your grandfather's is the southeast quarter of section 9."

"Where do I drive my stake?" asked Josh.

"Right by that small bush," answered John. "Then wait for your father and David."

Josh watched John ride off. Then he untied the stake from his saddle and climbed down from Lightning. With both hands, he pushed the stake deep into the ground. The 9th Kansas Cavalry flag waved in the breeze.

Josh walked over and hugged Lightning's neck. He took a cloth from the saddlebag. He wiped the white **lather** off the horse's body.

Then Josh sat in the shade. He waited for his father to arrive.

CHAPTER 8

Josh wiped the sweat from his face. He noticed his hands were black from the ashes.

Suddenly a man rode out of the bushes. He dismounted and drove a stake into the ground. Then he gave Josh a mean look.

"Better leave here, boy!" he snarled.

"But I was here first, mister," answered Josh. "My stake is over there."

The man walked over to Josh's stake. He kicked it over with his boot. Then he put his hands on his hips. He stared at Josh.

"I told you, boy," he yelled. "Move away from here!"

Josh was scared. But he slowly stood up. He walked closer to the man.

"But you don't understand, mister," Josh explained. "I drove my stake in first. This is my family's land."

Then Josh saw the man reach into his waistband. He pulled out a pistol.

But the man was interrupted by a lone rider. He dismounted next to them. The rider wore a western hat, pistol, and badge.

"Just drop the gun," the second man ordered.

"Says who?" growled the first man.

"Says Deputy U.S. Marshal Bill Tilghman. That's who!" replied the second man.

The first man let the pistol fall to the ground. "I was just trying to scare this young **claim jumper** away," he said.

The marshal looked at Josh. "Is that true, son?" he asked.

"No, sir, it isn't," answered Josh. "I staked the land first." He showed the marshal his flag.

"The kid didn't make the run," the man argued. "His horse isn't even lathered. Now look at mine. That's the proof."

"I've already wiped Lightning down," Josh explained.

Josh walked over to the man's horse. Something didn't look right.

Josh touched the white substance with his finger. Then he put his finger on the tip of his tongue.

"This isn't lather, marshal," said Josh. "This is white soap!"

Marshal Tilghman tasted it too. Then he ordered the man to leave or be arrested. The man jumped on his horse and fled.

The lawman waited with Josh. He met Josh's father when he and David finally arrived.

"I'm Deputy Marshal Bill Tilghman," he said. "You have a brave son, Mr. McCord. He stood up to a claim jumper. The **sooner** was hiding in the bushes."

"I'm proud of you, son," his father said.

"I'm in charge of the land office in Perry," said the marshal. "That town will soon become a boomtown. Ride with me. I'll be your witness when you file your claim."

Mr. McCord took the certificate and claim description from Josh. Then he mounted Lightning.

"I'll be back after our claim is filed," Mr. McCord said. Then he waved good-bye and rode off with the marshal.

Josh and David restaked the claim. Once again, the 9th Kansas Cavalry flag waved in the breeze.

CHAPTER 9

It was sunset of the next day. Josh McCord was very happy. Both homesteads now belonged to his family.

Joseph Eagle Claw's family had helped already. They had built two dugouts for the McCords. The dugouts were hidden in a low hill in the meadow. Josh's family would live in those while the **soddies** were built.

Joseph's many friends planned to help build the soddies before winter. The large one would be for Josh, his parents, and Jenny. And the smaller one would be for Grandpa and Uncle Nate.

A typical family in front of a sod house

Now Josh was sitting with his parents and Jenny. They were around a fire. It was in front of the covered wagon and animals.

"I'm so proud of you two," said Josh's mother. She was rocking Jenny in her lap.

"Josh deserves all the credit for the race," said Mr. McCord.

"But I think Lightning was the real hero, Pa," said Josh. "He won the race. I just rode along."

"But you talked to him from your heart. Right, son?" His father smiled. "And he ran faster for you. And he protected you."

Josh looked into his father's eyes. "That's right, Pa," he answered. "I talked to him from my heart."

Then Josh looked toward the red sunset. He could see Grandpa Henry, Joseph Eagle Claw, and Uncle Nate. They were standing together. And they had their arms around one another.

Josh knew this was the beginning of a new life!

NATIVE AMERICANS AND THE UNITED STATES GOVERNMENT

The United States government passed the Northwest Ordinance in 1787. It protected the Native Americans. Their rights could never be taken away. And their lands would always be theirs.

In 1789, about four million people lived in the U.S. They lived along the eastern coast.

Andrew Jackson was president in 1829. The United States had grown to about 12 million people.

Andrew Jackson

43

White settlers wanted to move west into the Native American lands. The government gave in.

A new law was passed in 1830. It forced southern Native Americans to move. They had to move west of the Mississippi River.

These people were the Cherokee, Chickasaw, Creek, Choctaw, and Seminole. They were known as the Five Civilized Tribes.

They had learned the white man's ways. They lived in log cabins. They wore **homespun** clothing. They tended livestock. They plowed fields with oxen. They even married whites.

Most leaders could read and write English. And most understood the law.

The Cherokee were the most advanced tribe. They refused to move.

They lived on farms in Tennessee, North Carolina, South Carolina, and Georgia. Some even owned black slaves.

In 1838, U.S. soldiers rounded up the Native Americans at gunpoint. They were forced to travel westward. This 800-mile journey was made in winter. Most Native Americans, young and old, had to walk.

On the way, one out of every four died. They died from **dysentery** and **measles**. They also died from **whooping cough** and starvation.

The Cherokee called this journey their Trail of Tears.

The Native Americans finally reached the Indian Territory. They continued to live in the white man's ways.

Their capital was in Tahlequah. They had a **democratic** government and a school system.

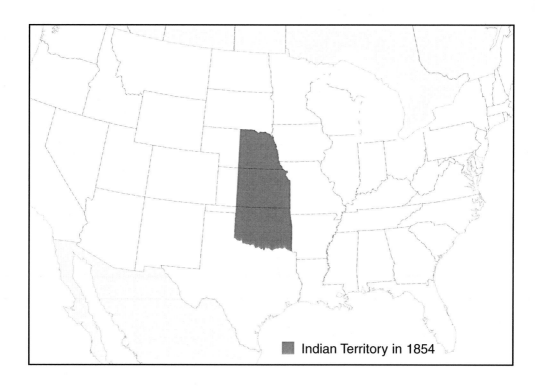

Indian Territory in 1854

The Cherokee created their own alphabet. They published a newspaper in English. They also published it in their own language. It was called the *Cherokee Advocate*.

The American Civil War took place from 1861 to 1865. It reached into the Indian Territory. Slave-holding Native Americans fought on the Confederate side. Others fought on the Union side.

Some remained **neutral**. They often fought against one another.

The Battle of Locust Grove was an important Union victory. It took place in the Indian Territory. The 1st Indian Home Guard, made up of loyal Cherokee, and the 9th Kansas Cavalry were Union regiments. They played an important role in the battle.

Many Native American lives were lost during the Civil War. The war destroyed much of their land and property.

By 1885, many white farmers wanted to move west. They wanted the rich Indian land.

The United States government had forced the Native Americans to sell their **surplus** land. They were paid about $1.40 per acre. Or they were given small homesteads as payment.

In 1889, the United States government opened Indian lands it had bought. Five land runs and a land **lottery** were scheduled.

President Jackson had promised the Native Americans that certain lands were to be owned "as long as the grass grows or the water runs." The government had forgotten its promise.

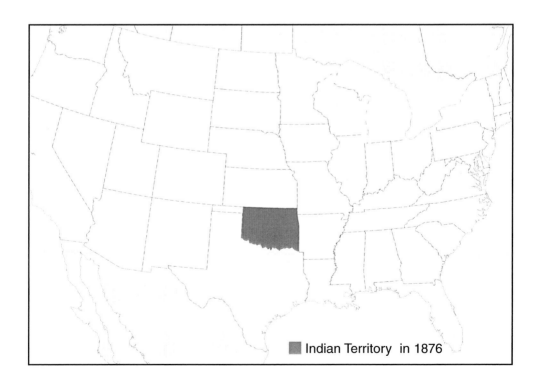

Indian Territory in 1876

OKLAHOMA LAND RUSHES

After the Civil War, eastern cities wanted good beef. This demand started the great cattle drives. Texas herds were driven to towns in Kansas. Then railroads shipped the cattle east.

OKLAHOMA
TERRITORY

INDIAN
TERRITORY

Oklahoma Land Openings

From 1865 to 1885, about 6 million head of cattle left Texas. Cowboys drove their longhorns on cattle trails. The Chisholm Trail was often used. It went through the Cherokee Strip. The trail ended in such Kansas towns as Wichita and Dodge City.

Eventually, cattlemen agreed to pay the Native Americans for letting their cattle graze on the rich grass on the Cherokee Strip.

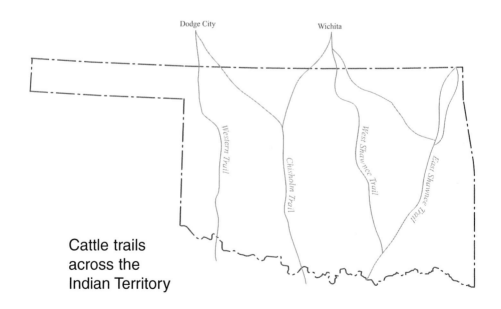

Cattle trails across the Indian Territory

Coal was also discovered in the Indian Territory. When railroads became important during the Civil War, that coal was needed as fuel.

Coal miners were given permission to enter Indian Territory. They were to teach the Native Americans how to mine coal.

In 1866, the government allowed railroads to cross Indian Territory. Large gangs of railroad workers came too.

Now more people wanted the Indian Territory opened for settlement. Cowboys and miners wrote letters. They told of the rich soil they had seen.

Railroads sent **pamphlets** to neighboring states. They told about the wonderful land. Settlers felt they should have the right to take it.

But it was the Boomers who made the strongest demand. They were an organized group of homesteaders led by David L. Payne. The group tried to claim the land many times. But each time, soldiers chased them out.

Most Indians wanted to keep their lands. But in time, they were forced to sell. The United States government gave them **allotments**. These were in the form of money or homesteads.

In 1889, President Benjamin Harrison issued a proclamation. It opened the Oklahoma and Indian Territories to settlement.

These Twin Territories would later become the state of Oklahoma.

On April 22, the first land rush took place. Homesteads of 160 acres and town lots could be claimed. Certain sections were reserved for schools.

Men had to be 21 years old to stake a claim. Unmarried women and widows were also allowed to claim land. All had to be U.S. citizens.

But people who already owned more than 160 acres could not claim additional land.

In 1881, a law was passed. It gave Civil War veterans Preference Rights. These rights let another adult make a claim for a Civil War veteran.

Land runs were made on horseback, in carriages, buggies, open wagons, and covered wagons. Some people went on foot and in slow-moving trains. Others even rode bicycles.

In each land rush, there were more people than available claims. So good horses were purchased.

People practiced before the race. Often, fast horses were stolen or purposely injured.

Settlers had to register for the land run. They would receive certificates. Then they would race for the land. Once they reached the desired land, they would drive a stake into the ground.

The settlers would take their certificates and claim descriptions to the nearest land office. There, they would register their claims.

The Cherokee Strip was the biggest land run. It took place on a very hot, dusty day, September 16, 1893.

About 100,000 land-hungry people heard the starting guns. They raced for about 40,000 homesteads and town lots.

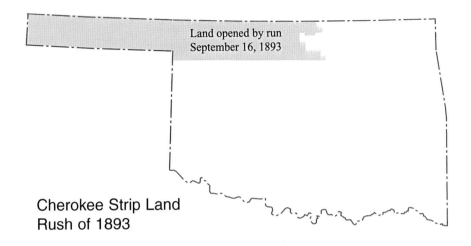

Land opened by run
September 16, 1893

Cherokee Strip Land
Rush of 1893

Certificates cost $14.00. Homestead fees ranged from $1.00 to $2.50 an acre. The better land was more expensive.

Often eager settlers sneaked across the starting line. They would hide near good claims. When the race began, they would come out and stake the claim. They were known as sooners. If caught, angry mobs often demanded they be killed.

Sometimes, more than one person claimed the same land. This resulted in fights and killings. Most fights were settled in land offices or in law courts.

BOOMTOWNS AND SODDIES

A boomtown is a town that has sudden growth. Normally, western towns took years to develop. During the Oklahoma land rushes, towns sprang up between noon and sunset.

At noon on April 22, 1889, no one lived in the towns of Guthrie and Oklahoma City. By evening, they both had populations of about 12,000 people.

During the Cherokee Strip Land Rush of 1893, it was much the same. The town of Perry and others were also born in a single afternoon.

These instant tent towns had many problems. They needed fresh water and garbage plans. Many needed **latrines** dug.

In some towns, streets had not been laid out. Often, the towns had no fire protection or law enforcement.

Sometimes, U.S. marshals and soldiers provided the law and order.

Once these problems were solved, family members came to join the homesteaders. Soon, tents were replaced with wooden buildings.

Bill Tilghman had been the marshal in Dodge City, Kansas. He retired and took part in the land rush of 1889. Later, he was appointed Deputy U.S. Marshal.

Tilghman helped enforce the law in the boomtowns of Guthrie, Perry, and Oklahoma City.

Bill Tilghman

Bill Tilghman was killed in the line of duty at age 70.

Marshal Tilghman had served as a peace officer for 50 years. This record was unequaled by any other western lawman.

Most homestead claims did not contain trees. Settlers learned to use the tough, prairie sod as a building material.

The top three inches of soil were held together by roots. These tangled roots of buffalo grass were thick and strong. Only the new steel plow, invented by John Deere in the 1860s, could cut through it.

Sod was cut into sections. It was stacked, like building blocks, for walls. Cracks were filled with mud.

Sod sections were also used on the roof. These prairie houses were called soddies. Settlers, or sodbusters, cut and laid these blocks. Sodbusters farmed the prairies.

Any available wood was used for the roof supports. Wood was also used to frame the doors and windows. The wood often came from the settlers' covered wagons.

The sod house was the homesteader's solution to the lack of building material on Oklahoma's treeless plains.

Many times, settlers lived in dugouts until their soddies were built. A dugout was made by digging a hole in the side of a low hill. Sometimes, families lived in their covered wagons during the building process.

Soddies were cool in the summer. And they were warm in the winter. But they were also dirty and dangerous. In a heavy rain, the roof could fall on the people inside.

Sod also attracted insects, rats, and snakes. Sometimes, insects fell from the ceiling. If the family was eating, these bugs would drop right into their food!

Most settlers built windmills to pump water from underground. And they used cow or buffalo **chips** for cooking fuel.

To keep the land, a homesteader had to farm a claim for five years. And he or she also had to improve it in some way. Improvements included a permanent house, a barn, a corral for animals, or crops. Then the homesteader would receive the legal deed to land.

But homesteaders suffered from droughts and blizzards. They also suffered through prairie fires, dust storms, and loneliness.

Many homesteaders left their Oklahoma claims. They often tried to sell their claims to their neighbors. They looked for places where living was easier.

But most remained on the land. They were determined to live the new life they had raced for.

GLOSSARY

allotment portion of something given as payment

amputate to cut off

cavalry army unit mounted on horses

certificate piece of paper issued at the starting booth. It was proof that a person had registered and could legally race. A claim could not be filed without a certificate and a claim description.

chip piece of dried manure

claim to take as one's own

claim jumper person who tries to take land away from the original owner

Confederate relating to the beliefs of the Southern states during the Civil War

democratic relating to a government controlled by the people

dysentery disease caused by an infection; severe diarrhea

gait foot movements by which a horse moves forward

gallop fast natural gait (see separate glossary entry) of a horse

gear equipment

halter rope or strap for leading or tying an animal. It usually fits on the head.

homespun handmade from cloth woven at home

homestead land acquired or settled under the homestead law. The homestead law gave the government the right to sell land it owned.

lather foam that forms on a horse's body when it is extremely sweaty

latrine place in the earth, such as a pit, used as a toilet

lottery drawing to determine the winners of something

measles contagious disease caused by a virus marked by distinct red circular spots on the skin

neutral not supporting either side of an issue

pamphlet short unbound printed publication with either a paper cover or no cover

pinned down surrounded and held down by gunfire with no means of escape

pinto horse or pony marked with patches of white

played out worn out or used up

reins straps fastened to a bit (part of a bridle that fits over a horse's head) used to control a horse

rich having plenty of material to supply plants with healthy food

soddy house built using squares of strong grass and roots cut from the prairie

sooner person settling on land in the early West before it was officially opened for settlement

stake a claim to have the right to something by placing stakes, as the law requires

surplus relating to an amount that is left over when a need is filled

tarp heavy piece of material used to protect objects in the open

Union relating to the beliefs of the Northern states during the Civil War

whooping cough contagious disease caused by bacteria, marked by convulsive cough

winded out of breath